FLEATECTIVES
CASE OF THE KIDNAPPED MANTIS

D1584628

Look out for more

FLEATECTIVES

adventures

CASE OF THE STOLEN NECTAR

CASE OF THE MISSING GLOW-WORMS

FLEATECTIVES
CASE OF THE KIDNAPPED MANTIS

MISSING

UG!

JONNY ZUCKER
ILLUSTRATED BY CHRIS JEVONS

First published in the UK in 2014 by Scholastic Children's Books
An imprint of Scholastic Ltd
Euston House, 24 Eversholt Street
London, NW1 1DB, UK
Registered office: Westfield Road, Southam, Warwickshire, CV47 0RA
SCHOLASTIC and associated logos are trademarks and/
or registered trademarks of Scholastic Inc.

Text copyright © Jonny Zucker, 2014
Illustrations copyright © Chris Jevons, 2014

The right of Jonny Zucker and Chris Jevons to be identified as the author and
illustrator of this work has been asserted by them.

Cover illustration © Chris Jevons, 2014

ISBN 978 1407 13696 7

A CIP catalogue record for this book is available from the British Library.

Printed and bound by CPI Group (UK) Ltd, Croydon, CR0 4YY
Papers used by Scholastic Children's Books
are made from wood grown in sustainable forests.

1 3 5 7 9 10 8 6 4 2

www.scholastic.co.uk

For Kenil-Earth Fly-Mary School

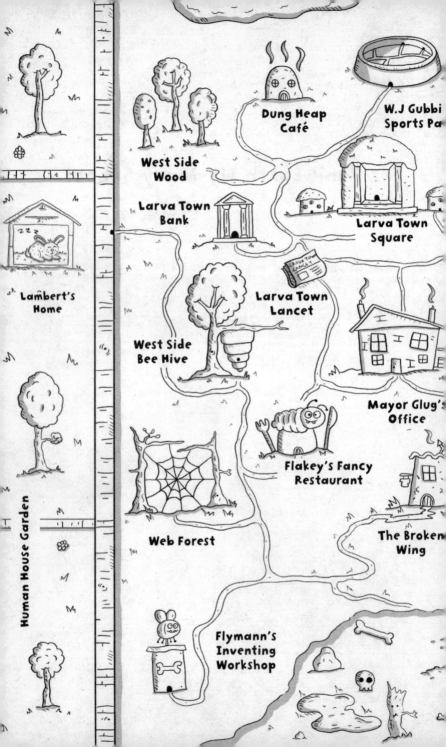

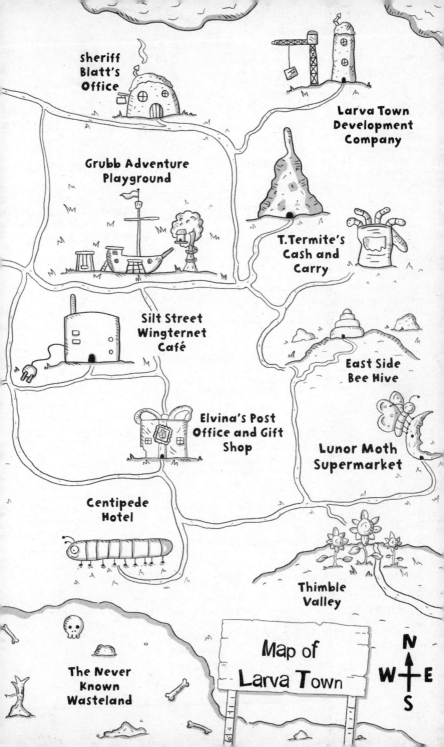

CHAPTER 1

It was late afternoon on a warm Sunday in West Side Wood, and Larva Town's two crime-crushing Fleatectives were taking things easy. Buzz was leaning back on a pine cone reading *The Crime-Crusher's Guide to Catching Bug*

Criminals, while Itch was studying a strange-looking tube stuck to a tree.

"I wonder what that is," murmured Itch, scratching his head. "It looks like part of some insect kids' treasure hunt."

Before Buzz could reply, a high-pitched shriek ripped through the air. Buzz leapt to his feet and ran in the direction of the scream.

"Wait for me!" called Itch.

Past the West Side Hive and the offices of the *Larva Town Lancet* the Fleatectives ran. They skidded to a halt outside Mayor Glug's headquarters, a large building made from blue stone and finely cut wooden blocks. Cedric and Octavia – the two fleas who worked for the mayor – were standing outside the building. They were sobbing, wailing and gnashing their mouth-parts.

"Hey, you guys, calm down and tell us what happened," said Buzz soothingly.

It took Cedric and Octavia a few moments to pull themselves together.

"It's this," sniffed Octavia, handing Buzz a piece of paper. It said:

Cedric + Octavia –

We have kidnapped your boss, the praying mantis Mayor Glug. We will hold on to him until you pay us one million Bug Notes – that's right – one million! You and Sheriff Blatt have until midnight on Tuesday to come up with the money. If you fail, you will never see the mayor again.

"What's the big deal?" asked Itch. "It's not as if the mayor's been kidnapped."

Buzz shot him a look.

"Oh," nodded Itch, looking at the note

again. "The mayor *has* been kidnapped."

"What are we going to do?" whimpered Octavia.

"We looked for Sheriff Blatt, but we couldn't find him," said Cedric sadly.

"Forget about the sheriff," said Itch. "He's probably watching some crummy crime show on Insect TV. Larva Town's two crime-crushing Fleatectives – that's me and Buzz – are here now. We're very experienced. We'll take this case. You've got nothing to worry about."

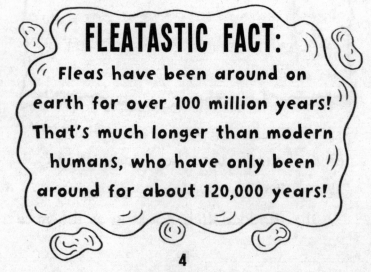

FLEATASTIC FACT:
Fleas have been around on earth for over 100 million years! That's much longer than modern humans, who have only been around for about 120,000 years!

"Nothing to worry about!" shouted Octavia. "Mayor Glug is the only insect around here who knows how to run Larva Town. He understands everything about the transport system, the hospitals and the schools. Without him everything will fall apart!" She and Cedric started sobbing again.

Itch put a claw on each of their shoulders.

"Do you two think you can keep the town running for a couple of days without Mayor Glug?" asked Buzz.

"I suppose so," sniffed Octavia, "but if anyone else finds out that he's been kidnapped, there'll be panic and pandemonium. Everyone relies on him."

"Then we're not going to tell anyone else," said Buzz. "You two get on with running the town and leave us to track down the kidnappers and get the mayor back."

"What?" cried Itch. "We're going to give them *one million* Bug Notes?"

"No way!" said Buzz firmly. "We'll rescue the mayor without paying them a penny."

"Pay who a penny for what?" asked a cockroach with a white letter "S" painted on his back. He strode up to the four fleas and eyed them suspiciously. It was Sheriff Blatt.

"Mayor Glug's been kidnapped," said Cedric.

"I thought we weren't going to tell anyone else!" protested Itch.

"It's OK," said Buzz. "Sheriff Blatt *is* the town's official law enforcer and he *was* mentioned in the ransom note."

"Yeah, but he's still rubbish," muttered

Itch under his breath.

"Look," said Octavia, handing the note to Blatt.

The sheriff snatched it, read it quickly and popped it in his mouth.

"I bet this is the work of The Painted Lady and Crustman," said Buzz.

"Definitely!" nodded Itch. "It smells of that exquisitely coloured but criminal butterfly and her violent woodlouse henchman!"

"It smells like nothing of the sort," said Sheriff Blatt, chewing the ransom note. "The Painted Lady and Crustman have been out of town for the last three days. They can't be connected to this kidnapping in any way."

"Drat!" said Itch.

"So what are we going to do?" asked Buzz.

"There is no *we*," said the sheriff. "*I'm*
in charge of this case and I have no need
of help from anyone else. This is what
I'm going to do: I'm going to go home
and watch *Stick Insect Thief Catchers*, and
think things over."

"But it's Sunday evening and the
kidnappers have set us a deadline of
midnight on Tuesday!" cried Itch.
"There's no time for watching Insect
TV – although *Earwig Kitchen Challenge* is
on tonight, and the last episode *was* fab."

"OK," sighed the sheriff, "I suppose
I'd better go and check out the mayor's
office to look for clues."

"We're coming too," said Buzz.

"If you must," sighed the sheriff. "Let's
just get it over with. Cedric and Octavia,
lead the way, please."

The five of them entered the building

and made their way past the first floor, where Cedric and Octavia worked. Mayor Glug's office was on the second floor. It was a large open room encircled by glass. To the left was his huge oak desk. At the far end were three plush grass sofas.

While Buzz and Itch started to comb the room for clues, Sheriff Blatt sat on one of the sofas and started whistling the theme tune from *Bugging Bug Crooks*.

"Er, how are you going to find any clues if you just sit down and whistle?" asked Itch.

"I don't need to look for clues," said the sheriff. "The clues come to me."

Itch rolled his eyes.

Ten minutes later, while Buzz and Itch were still searching, Sheriff Blatt stood up and announced that they had been there long enough. "There are no clues here," he said.

"But we've hardly looked!" protested Buzz.

"Everyone out!" commanded the sheriff. "I've already missed the start of *Stick Insect Thief Catchers* and I want to see the rest of it."

As soon as they were outside the mayor's office, Sheriff Blatt pulled out a long roll of black-and-yellow-striped crime tape and stuck it over the door.

"Cedric and Octavia, you can carry on working on the first floor," he said, "but the mayor's office is now a crime scene. No one goes in and no one comes out without my permission."

"Er . . . how could anyone come out if they can't go in?" asked Itch.

The sheriff ignored Itch and the five insects went back downstairs and outside into the fading light.

"Hey, look at that," cried Buzz, pointing to some of the wooden blocks on the outer walls of the building. In several places the wood had worn away.

"Must be the rain," said Octavia.

"A worn-away wall is a worn-away wall is a worn-away wall," scoffed Blatt. "It's not connected to this case in any way."

Buzz frowned.

"You're not going to pay the ransom money, are you, Sheriff?" asked Itch. "We think that's a really bad idea."

"The answer will float into my brain when I'm least expecting it," replied Blatt. "Now if you'll excuse me, I'm going back to my office for the night. Tomorrow afternoon I'll go and check out the mayor's home for clues. Cedric, Octavia – do you have a spare key for his apartment?"

Octavia fumbled in her pocket and pulled out a shiny key. Blatt took it, then turned to Buzz and Itch. "I suggest you two amateurs go home and leave the detective work to me."

"Grrrrrr!" seethed Itch.

And with that, Blatt turned and strolled off in the direction of his office and his beloved TV.

"No fair!" said Itch. "While he's busy watching TV, we could be getting on with cracking the case."

"I know," sighed Buzz. "The mayor's apartment is the right place to start looking for clues, but Blatt has the spare key so we can't get in."

"Er . . . you could always use this," said Octavia, pulling out an identical key to the one she'd just given Blatt.

"We had *two* spare keys cut," smiled Cedric.

Buzz's face lit up.

"To the mayor's luxury apartment!" cried Itch.

Can you find the missing words?

```
R Z A L F Z M Y K Q S A
I A E B A K J A K A M E
A M Y U G I Z U A E A P
B A T Z A D Z B I A Y X
C U X Z D N T A S H O O
H S G L R A N S O M R D
E G A N F P A U P R G A
P W L R O A H Q I A L N
K Y D U J T A I A B U A
J V Q K A M E C T W G O
A S M A N T I S A C A C
V F A W N X O B V G H Z
```

BUZZ	KIDNAP
ITCH	RANSOM
MAYOR GLUG	BUG NOTES
MANTIS	KEY

Answers at the back of the book

CHAPTER 2

Holding the key, Itch started shaking his body from side to side and twisting and turning his abdomen. Within a few seconds his whole body was a blur of crazy movement.

"Er . . . what's he doing?" asked
Octavia.

"He thinks he's going to be the
world's first flying flea," sighed Buzz,
whacking Itch on the back.

Itch abruptly stopped his mad
movements. "What did you do that for?"
he cried. "I was nearly flying that time!"

"No, you weren't," scolded Buzz.
"We're fleas, Itch. We jump. We don't
fly. End of story!"

Itch's face drooped sadly.

"But we're going to get inside the
mayor's apartment and do our best to
find some clues," added Buzz.

Itch brightened up.

"Do you really think you'll be able to
get Mayor Glug back without paying any
of the ransom money?" asked Octavia.

"Have no fear," said Itch, resting a leg

on Cedric's shoulder. "With Itch on the case, the mayor will be back before you can say 'mighty missing mantis'!"

"Mighty missing mantis," said Octavia.

There was no sign of the mayor.

"OK," said Itch, "he'll be back before you can say. . ."

Buzz clamped a claw over Itch's mouth-parts. "Thanks for the key," he said. "We'll be off now. Please try not to get too downhearted, and don't forget: tell no one about this, and keep things running as smoothly as possible until we get Mayor Glug back!"

"Do you think the town's wasps kidnapped the mayor?" asked Itch, as the Fleatectives hurried towards Glug's apartment. "Maybe they ran out of humans to sting and grabbed him instead?"

"Unlikely," replied Buzz. "There are quite a lot of humans out there."

"What about ants? They work in big groups and can carry really heavy things."

"We'd have seen or heard them," replied Buzz.

"Well, how about Cedric and Octavia? Maybe they're pretending to be upset, but in reality they kidnapped Glug because they want to become mayor themselves?"

"Cedric and Octavia are totally loyal to the mayor," said Buzz. "That wailing and shouting back there was for real. They're very, very upset by this. Plus, they gave us the key. They want us to solve the case."

By the time they'd reached the mayor's place it was dark. The apartment was made largely from wood and Buzz went to inspect some of the sections where the wood had been worn away.

"Interesting," he murmured.

While he was doing that, Itch struggled with the key. He twisted it and turned it. Finally, he started bashing the door with his feet.

"It's no good," said Itch. "It must be the wrong key."

"You've got it upside down," said Buzz.

"Oh," said Itch, going red. He turned the key the right way round and opened the door. The apartment was eerily dark. The only light was provided by the night's silvery moon drifting in through the windows. The fleas checked the downstairs floor as quietly as they could. They saw a twig cupboard, a couple of bark sofas and a collection of *The Mayor* magazines,

but not a clue was in sight.

Buzz nodded towards the staircase. They crept up it slowly, Itch holding on to one of Buzz's legs. At the top of the stairs was a corridor with a room at either end. A strip of light was shining under the door of the room on the left.

They inched towards the room. Buzz nudged the door open and they peered around it cautiously. Inside were a small pebble cupboard, a chair and a round writing table. Two lit candles rested on the table.

"Why is there a light on when the mayor's not here?" whispered Itch nervously.

Buzz shrugged his shoulders and they stepped over to the table. On it was a newspaper cutting from an old copy of the *Larva Town Lancet*.

LARVA TOWN LANCET

The only newspaper you can eat

MAYOR CLOSES DIRT SHACK RESTAURANT

Yesterday Larva Town's Mayor Glug shut down the Dirt Shack Restaurant. When he arrived to inspect the eaterie, he found bark sap mixed with soil juice, mouldy grass stains on the kitchen floor and knives and forks that were being stored in the mouth of an ant-eater with the flu. Recently there have been many reports of insects getting food poisoning after eating at the Shack.

"Every insect likes a bit of dirt, especially a praying mantis like me," said the mayor, "but the Dirt Shack went too far. I have made the decision to close it down for good."

FLEATASTIC FACT:

Praying mantises love meat and feed on other insects. They particularly love eating animals that are bigger than them, like birds, small frogs and lizards!

"Do you think this story is connected to the kidnapping?" asked Buzz.

"Nah," replied Itch. "The kidnappers haven't asked for food as a ransom, they've asked for money."

"Good point," nodded Buzz.

That moment they heard a noise out in the corridor.

The Fleatectives looked at each other, then tiptoed back to the door. They glanced out. A shadow darted into the room at the other end of the corridor.

"Maybe the kidnappers are holding Mayor Glug here," whispered Itch.

"Let's check it out," nodded Buzz.

Slowly they edged along the hallway. The other room was dark.

The two Fleatectives puffed out their chests and adopted insect martial arts positions. Buzz's stance was a real one he'd learned at insect martial arts school. Itch's was a stance he'd just made up.

They reached the door. Buzz took the handle in his claws. He mouthed, "One . . . two . . . three," and flung open the door.

In a flash, a creature shot out between the Fleatectives, zoomed along the corridor and sped down the stairs.

"Stop!" yelled Buzz.

He and Itch jumped down the stairs and threw themselves in the direction of the creature. Itch completely missed and went crashing head first into a wall. Buzz's attack was more accurate. He landed right on top of the creature with a rousing yell of "*Gotcha!*"

Can you match the keys to the correct locks?

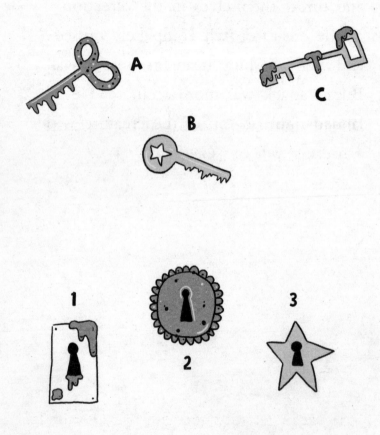

Answers at the back of the book

CHAPTER 3

"Don't hurt me!" squeaked the creature from underneath Buzz.

It was a terrified-looking grey moth. Its compound eyes were blinking nervously, its mandibles shaking from side to side.

"Where are you hiding Mayor Glug?"

demanded Itch, rubbing his sore head. "Is he under one of your wings?"

"No," said the moth, opening his wings to show that there was no mayor concealed inside. "My name's Hector. I'm Mayor Glug's housekeeper."

"Where do you keep his house?" asked Itch.

"No, Itch," sighed Buzz, getting off the moth. "Hector cooks and cleans and tidies this apartment for the mayor. Why did you run away from us, Hector?"

"I thought you were burglars. I didn't want you to find me."

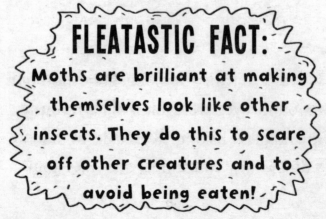

FLEATASTIC FACT:
Moths are brilliant at making themselves look like other insects. They do this to scare off other creatures and to avoid being eaten!

"We're not burglars!' cried Itch. "We're crime-crushing fleas!"

"Then why are you here? What crime has been committed?" asked Hector.

"Mayor Glug has been kidnapped and we found a ransom note demanding one million Bug Notes," said Buzz.

"I thought we weren't going to tell anyone else!" complained Itch.

"It's fine to tell Hector because he works for the mayor," said Buzz. "Now, what can you tell us about the mayor's recent movements?"

"Mayor Glug is a mantis of habit," said Hector anxiously. "The only two places he ever goes are this apartment and his office. It's a fifteen-minute walk between them. He leaves here in the morning at 7.45 a.m. and gets to his office at exactly 8 a.m. He leaves his office at 7.45 p.m.

and gets home on the dot of 8 p.m."

"So the only places he could have been kidnapped are either of those locations or somewhere on the walk between them," said Buzz.

Hector frowned.

"What is it?" asked Itch.

"Well, there have been several occasions in the last few weeks when he's got home later, around 9 p.m. I was a bit worried because he's so fussy about sticking to his timings."

"Maybe he just stayed at work for an extra hour," suggested Buzz.

Hector shook his head. "I didn't want to be rude and ask the mayor directly, but I know Cedric and Octavia so I asked them."

"What did they say?" asked Itch.

"They said he leaves work at exactly

7.45 p.m. every single day. He never leaves later."

"So we don't know what he was doing between 7.45 p.m. and 9 p.m. on those occasions?" asked Buzz.

"Correct," Hector replied.

"What about friends?" asked Itch. "Who does the mayor like to hang out with?"

"His only real friend is Larva Town's doctor, Dr Bopper."

Buzz and Itch had seen Bopper a couple of times. He was an old and wise carpet beetle who liked to take things very slowly.

"OK," nodded Buzz. "It's too late to see Bopper tonight but we'll go find him first thing in the morning."

"Thanks for your help," said Itch, "and please don't tell anyone else about the mayor being kidnapped."

"Of course not," said Hector nervously. "I hope you find him soon."

"This is way too early for me!" complained Itch, rubbing his eyes as he and Buzz walked towards Larva Town Square early the following morning.

They'd both slept for a few hours on their home rabbit, Lambert, but with less than forty-eight hours until the kidnappers' Tuesday midnight deadline, they had to come up with some clues as to Mayor Glug's whereabouts – and fast.

No one else was awake and the sun was just starting to rise as they reached the huge Square. At one end was a giant bandstand flanked on either side by mushroom–stool music speakers. To the left was the town's Tourist Information Bureau. To the right was a craft fair that wouldn't be open for a few hours.

Dr Bopper was meditating on one of the square's many twig benches and chanting some unrecognizable words when the Fleatectives approached him.

"Dr Bopper," said Itch, tapping the carpet beetle on the head.

"What . . . ?" blurted out Bopper, his

eyes snapping open.

"Sorry for the intrusion," said Buzz, "but we're the town's crime-crushing Fleatectives and we'd like to ask you some questions."

"Medical questions?" asked the doctor.

"No," said Buzz, lowering his voice. "Questions about Mayor Glug. He's been kidnapped."

"I thought we weren't going to tell anyone else!" protested Itch.

"This is the mayor's best friend," pointed out Buzz. "He may have some clues for us."

"That is terrible news," said Bopper. "Did the kidnappers leave a ransom note?"

"They want one million Bug Notes in exchange for his safe return," said Itch.

"We spoke to his housekeeper, Hector, last night," said Buzz, "and he said you're the mayor's only real friend."

"That's true," nodded Bopper. "He's not a great one for seeing other insects and going to parties."

"Have you noticed anything odd recently?" asked Buzz. "Has the mayor been acting strangely? Has anyone been following him? Has he been upset?"

Dr Bopper stroked his chin thoughtfully. "Well, he wasn't too happy about the diet I put him on."

"Why did you put him on a diet?" asked Itch.

"He was eating too much junk food, particularly his favourites – Mouldy Curl Chilli Snacks. They're expensive and very difficult to get hold of, but he adores them. I said they were bad for his digestion. I told him to stop eating them at once."

"How did he react to your ban?" asked Buzz.

"He didn't take it too well," replied Bopper. "He said he would really miss them. But he knew I would keep bugging him about it, so he agreed to cut them out and start eating healthier foods."

"Anything else you can think of?" asked Itch.

The doctor shook his head.

"Well, thanks for that info," said Buzz. "Could you get in touch with us if anything else does pop into your head?" He handed Dr Bopper a Fleatectives business card.

"Certainly," nodded the carpet beetle, arranging himself back into his meditation pose and starting to chant again.

"What do you think?" asked Buzz as the Fleatectives walked back across the

Town Square.

"I think he's a beetle doctor who likes meditating," replied Itch.

"No," sighed Buzz, "I mean about what he told us. Hector mentioned that the mayor has gone missing for an hour or so a few times, and the doctor told us he recently banned the mayor from eating junk food."

"So?" said Itch.

"So, the missing hours might have been spent going to some out-of-the-way place where he could get his legs on some Mouldy Curl Chilli Snacks without Dr Bopper knowing about it."

"The only out-of-the-way eating place I can think of that might serve such a snack is the Dung Heap Café," replied Itch.

"Exactly," nodded Buzz. "That's why we're going there right now."

Fill in the missing letters

1. H _ C _ O _

2. D _ _ OPP _ _ _

3. M _ _ _ _ _ D _ _ _ U _ L
   C _ _ _ _ LI _ NA _ K _

4. _ U _ G _ E _ P C _ _ E

5. M _ _ _ _ _ R _ L _ _ _

6. _ LE _ _ EC _ _ _ VE _

Answers at the back of the book

CHAPTER 4

"Wouldn't it be great if we got to the café and the mayor was just sitting there eating junk food?" said Itch, as they strode through a leafy glade.

"It would be," agreed Buzz, "but then why would someone write a ransom note?"

"Oh, yeah," nodded Itch, "I hadn't thought of that."

The door of the Dung Heap Café was a barred archway. On the first floor were two round barred windows. Together they looked like a scary face staring out.

Buzz pushed the door. It opened with a creak.

The Fleatectives stepped into the dark interior. The café was a round space with a serving counter at the far end leading off to a kitchen.

A hazy fog filled the air along with the strong, but not unpleasant, smell of frying bark. On one wall was a blackboard listing the day's specials.

Twice-fried Oil soup
with EXTRA oil

Tooth-rot seed cakes

Stomach-BURNING
SOUR berry BURGERS

"This really is the place for junk food," murmured Buzz.

"Delicious," drooled Itch.

A series of mud tables and chairs were set out around the room. There were only two customers. A goofy-looking bee sat at one table, furiously eating her way through a huge pile of Juicy Beet Fries. A small grasshopper was sitting at another table sipping from a tall glass of Greasy Stalk Elixir.

Buzz and Itch nodded at the customers and strolled over to the serving counter. On it were several brightly coloured packets of Mouth-part Wrecker Bubblegum.

"Hello!" Itch called in the direction of the kitchen.

After a few moments the door opened and a smiling female tapeworm slid out. She had a long, ribbon-shaped body split into sections and large oval eyes.

FLEATASTIC FACT:
There are over 6,000 different types of tapeworm on planet earth! They climb into food and spread disease so it's best to avoid them!

"What can I get for you gents?" she grinned.

"Are you the owner of this junk-food establishment?" asked Buzz.

"Indeed I am," replied the tapeworm. "They call me Spicy Flaxton."

"They may call you that, but what's your name?" asked Itch.

"Spicy Flaxton," she replied.

Itch looked confused.

"We were wondering if Mayor Glug has been here recently," said Buzz.

"I wish he had been," sighed Spicy, shaking her head. "It would have been great for business. . . You know: '*Mayor enjoys delicacies at Larva Town's premier eating spot.*' Times have been tough recently."

"So he's never even popped in?"

"No," said Spicy sadly.

"Have you served any Mouldy Curl Chilli Snacks in the past few weeks?" asked Itch. "They're the mayor's favourites."

"I'm afraid not," said Spicy. "I can't get my hands on any of the Mouldy Curl range at the minute; it seems like there aren't any in Larva Town. Do you guys know where I can buy some?"

"I'm afraid not," replied Itch. "We only dine at Lambert the rabbit. That's where we live."

"Too bad," said Spicy. "Let me know if you come across any."

"Will do," nodded Itch.

"Well," sighed Buzz, "if the mayor hasn't visited here and you haven't been selling those snacks, we'd better be moving on."

"Sorry I couldn't be of more help," said Spicy.

As she turned to go, Itch spotted a small green patch on her neck.

"Is that a tattoo?" he asked.

Spicy frowned, then realized what Itch was pointing at. "Oh, that," she laughed. "Um . . . yes, I had it done last week. Green's my favourite colour."

"Mine too," beamed Itch.

"Come on," said Buzz, looking carefully at the tattoo. "We need to keep searching for clues."

The Fleatectives left the dim interior of the café and walked back out into the daylight.

"Hey, check that out," said Itch, pointing to a tree. "There's another one of those tube things. The kids around here must be playing one giant treasure hunt. The tubes must be markers or something."

"Forget the tubes," said Buzz, "It's already Monday lunchtime and we've got nothing to go on."

"So what do we do next?" asked Itch.

"I say we head over to Sheriff Blatt's office. He's had long enough to watch TV and start his investigation. Maybe he's dug up some clues."

"Maybe or maybe not," huffed Itch. "That cockroach's work rate is slow, slow, slow."

When they arrived at the sheriff's office, they headed straight round the back to where the TV was located. Looking through a window, they could see Blatt fast asleep on a big sofa. The TV was showing *Butterfly Breakout Jail*. It took the Fleatectives a few minutes of banging on the window before they woke Blatt up. He shook himself groggily and reluctantly let them in.

"What do you two amateurs want?" he asked, rubbing his eyes.

"We wanted to see if you've found any clues at the mayor's apartment or anywhere else," said Itch, deliberately failing to mention that he and Buzz had already checked out the apartment themselves.

"I've unearthed loads of stuff," replied the sheriff.

"Such as?" asked Buzz.

"Exactly the same things as you two have uncovered."

"You have no idea what we've uncovered," said Itch.

"I can see into your minds," said Blatt. "Only a very experienced law enforcement insect can do that."

Buzz was about to reply, when Itch suddenly started shaking his body from side to side and hopping around.

"Please, Itch!" cried Buzz. "This is no time for flying attempts!"

As Itch's moves got faster and more bizarre, he nodded his head at Buzz and then pointed towards the floor.

While Sheriff Blatt watched Itch's
crazy movements, Buzz looked at the
floor where Itch had pointed. A small
piece of paper was lying there. In an
instant, Buzz had picked it up and
hidden it under his claw.

Itch abruptly stopped his flying practice.

"We've got to go now, Sheriff," he panted.

"Good," replied Sheriff Blatt, "I have an episode of *Modern Moth Muggings* to watch."

Once outside, Itch said, "I saw that paper being pushed under Blatt's door and noticed it said something about Mayor Glug. So I did my flying thing to distract Blatt and let you grab it."

"Superb work!" cried Buzz.

Itch glowed with insect pride.

They quickly read the note.

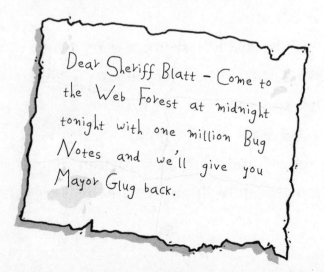

Dear Sheriff Blatt – Come to the Web Forest at midnight tonight with one million Bug Notes and we'll give you Mayor Glug back.

"It's the same handwriting that was on the ransom note!" Buzz exclaimed. "It's from the kidnappers. They said the ransom money was due on Tuesday night in their first note."

"But tonight's *Monday* night," pointed out Itch.

"I guess they've changed their minds," said Buzz. "We'll go there at midnight, say we have the cash and then snatch the mayor back. Case closed."

"What do you know about the Web Forest?" asked Itch. "It sounds pretty scary."

"It's probably just got a scary name," replied Buzz. "Let's go and ask Lambert what she knows about it."

"Agreed," nodded Itch.

After hours of failing to find *any* clues, it felt as if the Fleatectives might finally be getting somewhere with the case. With hearts full of hope and excitement, they raced back to their rabbit home.

Which one is the odd one out?

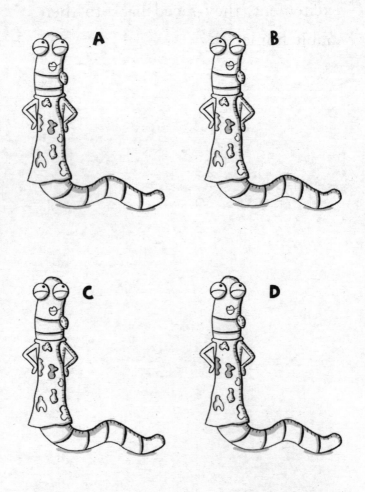

Answers at the back of the book

CHAPTER 5

Lambert lived at the bottom of a human family's garden. Her fur made a very comfy and warm bed for the Fleatectives.

Lambert spent most of her days and nights sleeping. When she wasn't sleeping, she was yawning, stretching or thinking about sleeping. The Fleatectives didn't know why she was so tired all of the time – it wasn't as if she actually *did* anything. Sure enough, when Buzz and Itch reached her, Lambert was fast asleep. They both took a big bite of her flesh, which woke her up.

"I've told you two not to bite me!" she snapped, opening one eye.

"And we've told you we only do it when we're hungry," said Itch. "There's no bad feeling involved."

"My skin gets a bad feeling every time you do it," winced the rabbit, slowly opening her other eye.

"Well, we're sorry," said Itch, "but we need to pick your brains."

"You're not going to bite my brain as well!" cried Lambert.

"No," said Buzz. "What we mean is, we have a question for you. What do you know about the Web Forest?"

"Well, it's mainly spiders who hang out there, but other types of insects do sometimes use it as a meeting place. It's a quiet spot to trade information or items."

"That makes sense," nodded Buzz.

"I should warn you that some of the spiders there don't take too kindly to non-spider visitors," said Lambert.

"I hope they don't know that we were the ones who put those villainous spiders, Alfie and Ma Rocks, in jail," shivered Itch.

"Worry not," said Buzz. "We'll be extra careful."

"But it sounds very dangerous,"
whimpered Itch.

"It's our only lead," replied Buzz.
"We're going!"

They set out half an hour before
midnight. A crescent moon hung in
a purple-black sky. Some owl babies
cheeped in a tree nearby. The snore of
an old wasp rippled through the air.

Itch tried everything he could to hinder the journey. He dived head first into a ditch and said he was drowning, even though there was no water in it. He fell on to the ground and said he had sunstroke, even though the sun had gone in hours ago. He hid inside a tree trunk and said he was afraid of wide-open spaces.

But Buzz would not be put off, and eventually they reached the Web Forest.

"Let's go over the plan," said Buzz.

"OK," replied Itch, his eyes darting nervously in all directions. "When we're a little way into the forest I do an impression of Sheriff Blatt's voice. This will make the kidnappers come towards me because they'll think I'm the sheriff and that I have the million Bug Notes. Before they reach me, you grab Mayor

Glug from them and we race out of the forest as fast as we possibly can. The mayor will be free, and we'll have handed the kidnappers nothing."

"Perfect," said Buzz. "Unfortunately, it will probably mean that the kidnappers will get away. But rescuing Mayor Glug is our number one priority."

The Web Forest was – unsurprisingly – surrounded by and covered in spider webs. Some were small, some were big, some were thin, some were thick; all were . . . webby.

"This can't be the right place," said Itch, pretending he couldn't see any webs.

"This way," said Buzz, pushing through a massive web and entering the forest.

Itch gulped and hurried after his partner.

Many of the webs were empty,
but a few had spiders at their centre.
Thankfully, they were all asleep.

"What do we do if the spiders all wake
up at the same time and try to gobble us
up in their silky webs?" whispered Itch,
his insides bubbling with fear.

FLEATASTIC FACT:
Most spiders make their
webs out of silk. They use the
silk to attract and capture
their prey!

"They're too tired," Buzz whispered
back.

They took a few paces further into
the forest. Itch was just about to start
his Blatt impression when they heard a
distant, high-pitched voice sing out: "This

way, Sheriff Blatt. We're over here. And we have the mayor. You'd better have the money."

Buzz and Itch looked through the darkness. They couldn't see anyone or anything, just hundreds of webs stretching into the distance.

"It's the kidnappers," whispered Buzz. "Do your Blatt voice, Itch."

"Sheriff Blatt here," announced Itch in a good copy of Blatt's voice. "Why don't you come over here so we can talk things through?"

"It would be better if you came this way," sang out the voice.

"I'll tell you what," called Itch as Blatt. "Let's meet halfway."

"That's a delightful idea," trilled the voice. "You take ten steps, we'll take ten steps and then we'll do the handover."

"One step," whispered Itch, as he and Buzz sidestepped a giant, crusty web hanging from a branch. "Two," he said as they walked on to a large, grey web lying on the ground. But Itch never got the chance to say "three", because the web gave way and the two Fleatectives went crashing into an enormously dark and fantastically deep hole.

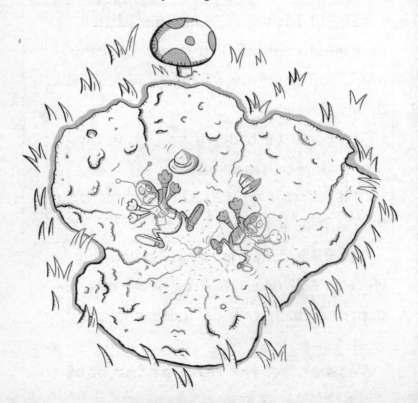

Help Buzz and Itch find their way to Web Forest.

START

FINISH

Web Forest

Answers at the back of the book

CHAPTER 6

"AAARRRGGGHHHH!" shrieked the Fleatectives as they hurtled downwards.

A second later they smacked on to a hard, muddy floor.

"Are you OK?" asked Buzz, rubbing his sore back.

"I think I'm dead," moaned Itch, stroking his claws.

"I can't believe it!" fumed Buzz. "I thought we'd trick them with your Blatt impression, but they tricked *us* with their falling-into-a-disguised-hole trick."

"I don't want to say I warned you it would be too dangerous," said Itch.

"BUT I WARNED YOU IT WOULD BE TOO DANGEROUS!!!"

"We should have left that note for Blatt. Then it would be him down here, not us," groaned Buzz. "The kidnappers think they've just trapped Blatt!"

The Fleatectives gingerly got to their feet and inspected their surroundings. All they could see were some strands of web covering the top of the hole. Buzz put a foot against one of the walls. It was incredibly sticky. He had to pull very hard at his leg to prise it away.

"This is bad," said Itch. "No – make that terrible. We're in a deep pit with sticky walls in a terrifying spider-web forest without any means of escape."

"Don't panic," said Buzz.

"Oh, and there's something else," said Itch, panicking like crazy. "In a few

69

hours, all of those sleeping spiders will wake up and realize there are two juicy fleas right in the middle of their forest!"

"They won't be able to get near us," said Buzz. "If we can't climb up the sticky walls they won't be able to walk down them."

"Good thinking," said Itch.

"Thanks," said Buzz glumly.

"Hey," said Itch, "there's another one of those weird tube things on the wall. Those treasure-hunt clues are everywhere!"

Buzz walked over to inspect the tube. "I have a funny feeling that these tubes aren't connected to a treasure hunt," he said thoughtfully. "I think they might be clues for the kidnapping case."

"But what are they?" asked Itch.

"No idea," sighed Buzz. "Let's try to get some sleep. Maybe in the morning when the sun is up we'll be able to see a way out of here."

The Fleatectives found it very difficult to sleep. Itch kept crying out, "Spiders of Doom!" while Buzz couldn't get comfortable. They finally managed to nod off at 3 a.m.

As soon as Itch opened his eyes, Buzz grabbed his antennae and dragged him to the darkest part of the hole.

"What are you doing?" hissed Itch.

Buzz pointed upwards with one of his claws. Itch followed the claw and saw seven huge spiders peering down into the hole. Itch wanted to scream, but Buzz put a foot over his mouth. After five minutes of looking, the spiders got bored and slunk off.

The Fleatectives spent the morning, the afternoon and the evening looking for a way out of the hole, but found nothing. It got dark. It got even darker. And then it got even darker still.

"It's about 9 p.m.," groaned Buzz, looking up at the moon shining into the hole. "We have just three hours until the kidnappers' original deadline. We're stuck down here. Sheriff Blatt won't capture the kidnappers and he certainly won't be able to raise one million Bug Notes. We have to face facts, Itch. We'll never see Mayor Glug again."

Itch was playing "tag" with himself, but this was proving difficult. As he tagged himself and fell on to a small mound of moss, he felt something hard dig into his belly. He moved the moss and found a couple of twigs.

"Look at me, Buzz!" he shouted, picking up the twigs and using them as stilts to wobble round the floor. "I'm a stick insect!"

Buzz looked up and his mouth suddenly fell open. He leapt up, grabbed the stilts from Itch and carried them to one of the walls. To his delight, when he pushed the first twig against the wall it stuck. He stuck the second twig next to it. Slowly he climbed up the two twigs.

Prising the twigs off the wall he stuck them back on but higher up, climbing with them.

"You're a genius, Itch!" he shouted. "I've made a ladder with your stilts!"

"I always knew I was a genius!" beamed Itch, running over to the wall.

Buzz carefully climbed up the twigs, until he reached the top of the hole. Quietly he crept out and threw the twigs down to Itch. Itch took them and started making his own ladder. A couple of minutes later he joined Buzz up on the surface. To their right was a group of massive spiders discussing the latest spider football results.

"OK," said Buzz. "The only way out is to run past that group."

"You can't be serious!" hissed Itch.

"Watch me," replied Buzz, launching himself forwards. Itch groaned and ran after his friend. They were in luck: the spiders were so heavily involved in their

conversation that they didn't notice the fleas sprinting past them.

"Time's running out," panted Buzz, as they left the Web Forest behind them. "I say we rush back to Mayor Glug's office and take another look for clues. Sheriff Blatt hurried us the first time, so we didn't get a chance to find anything."

As quick as they could, the Fleatectives raced towards the mayor's office. They were almost there when a figure blocked their path.

"Sheriff Blatt!" said Buzz.

"Where are you boys off to in such a hurry?" demanded the sheriff suspiciously.

"We're doing exercises for our special flea fitness regime," replied Buzz, throwing himself on to the ground and doing a couple of insect press-ups.

"Yeah!" nodded Itch, "we're going to be

the fittest fleas for miles around." He flexed his leg and displayed a very puny muscle.

"How are you doing with the mayor's case?" asked Buzz, getting back to his feet. "The deadline's nearly here."

"I found one million Bug Notes in Mayor Glug's office in a drawer marked *'emergencies'*," said the cockroach proudly.

"You can't hand that money over!" cried Buzz. "That will be letting the kidnappers win! We want to show them that crime doesn't pay!"

"If we want Mayor Glug back, that's the only way we're going to do it!" snapped the sheriff. "Now if you don't mind, I need to go back to my office, count the money again, watch *Worm City Crime Fiends* and then set out to meet the kidnappers. They sent me a note with the meeting place for the handover."

"Where is it?" demanded Buzz.

"As if I'd tell you two amateurs!"
scoffed the Sheriff, starting to walk away.

"We'd tell you!" shouted Itch, but
Blatt had gone.

"Luckily Blatt isn't like other
cockroaches," said Itch. "They're fast; he's
slow."

FLEATASTIC FACT: Cockroaches are incredibly fast. Once all of its six legs are moving, a cockroach can scuttle at eighty centimetres per second!

"Exactly," nodded Buzz. "That means there's still time for us to crack this case and stop the kidnappers before the sheriff makes a massive mistake!"

As they hurried to the mayor's office, they went over all that they knew about the case so far.

"Why are those weird tube things everywhere we go?" asked Buzz.

"What about Spicy Flaxton's green tattoo?" said Itch. "I saw you looking at it suspiciously."

"Hmm. I'm not sure it was a tattoo. It didn't look right, somehow. But I'm more concerned about the chunks of wood missing from the mayor's office and his apartment walls," nodded Buzz. "That doesn't seem right either."

"But how are they all connected?" demanded Itch.

Buzz shrugged his shoulders. "I don't know," he replied.

A short while later they arrived back at Glug's office. They hurried up the stairs past the first floor. Edging and twisting their way round the crime tape, they sneaked into his office.

"OK," whispered Buzz. "Let's check everywhere. I'm convinced there'll be another clue here."

While Itch checked the armchairs and cupboards, Buzz investigated the walls and floor. Half an hour later they'd uncovered . . . nothing. They moved on to investigate the mayor's desk, rifling through papers and photos and notes from lots of different meetings. There was absolutely nothing of any use. They were about to give up, when Buzz spotted a tiny button at the very back of one of the desk's drawers. He pushed it. There was a click and a tiny compartment suddenly fell open.

In the compartment was an order note that said:

WANT TO GET YOUR CLAWS ON SOME OF THOSE TERRIBLY RARE MOULDY CURL CHILLI SNACKS?

WELL, LOOK NO FURTHER!

WE AT T. TERMITE'S CASH &
CARRY EMPORIUM CAN GET HOLD
OF SOME AND DELIVER THEM
DIRECT TO YOUR DOOR.

At the bottom of the page, it added that the Emporium had recently sold a large batch of the snacks to the Dung Heap Café.

"Spicy Flaxton lied to us!" gasped Itch. "She said she hadn't served any of those snacks for ages. We need to go back there!"

"The café will be closed now," said Buzz. "It's 10.30 p.m. There's hardly any time left till the deadline! We must stop Blatt handing over that money. The kidnappers aren't exactly trustworthy. They will probably take the cash and *not* hand back the mayor."

Itch groaned in despair.

"However," said Buzz, "cash and carry places often stay open till late. Let's go and check out the Emporium."

A few seconds later Buzz and Itch were racing towards T. Termite's Cash and Carry Emporium.

"We'd better find something there," said Itch.

"I agree," nodded Buzz. "This is our very last chance to crack this case."

Which path leads to T. Termite's Cash and Carry Emporium?

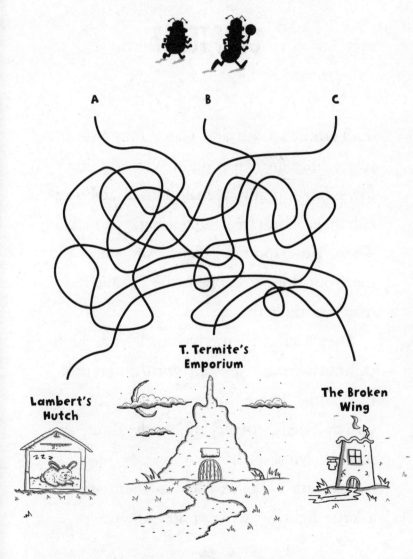

Answers at the back of the book

CHAPTER 7

T. Termite's Cash and Carry Emporium
was a huge brown mound with a pointy
tower on top and a small, closed archway
entrance. The place looked dark and still.
Then, Buzz spotted a light. And since
the front door was open, the Fleatectives
marched right in.

They found themselves in a vast, high-
ceilinged room, stacked with different
foodstuffs. There were mountains of
Crusty Seeds, towers of Nettle Bites, and
piles of Mud Tea.

Standing with his back to them was
a large light-brown termite. He was

studying something in a large orange crate.

Buzz coughed.

The termite turned around. He had
two pairs of long wings, curved antennae,
a broad waist and small eyes.

"Are you the 'T' in T. Termite's
Emporium?" asked Buzz.

"Yeah, I'm Tony," said the termite.
"What do you want?"

"We found an order note from your establishment in the mayor's office," said Itch. "It said you recently provided a local café with some Mouldy Curl Chilli Snacks."

"There must have been a mistake on the note," said Tony firmly. "I haven't sold any of those to the Dung Heap Café for ages."

"Thank you for your time," nodded Buzz, grabbing Itch and steering him straight outside.

"What are you doing?" demanded Itch when they were outside. "We only just started questioning him."

"Didn't you hear it?" said Buzz. "I only mentioned that it was a local café he'd been supplying. He immediately mentioned the Dung Heap Café by name. He knew exactly what we were talking about and he's lying through his termite teeth! And I spotted some green marks on his shoulder, just like Spicy Flaxton's supposed tattoo. But there's no way a termite would get a tattoo — they don't like any marks on them at all."

FLEATASTIC FACT: In spite of spending loads of time moving around in dirt, termites are very clean creatures that spend lots of time grooming each other!

"Look, Buzz," cried Itch. "There's another one of those tubes on a tree. And another. And another."

They rushed over to inspect the tubes.

Buzz bashed himself on the forehead. "I can't believe I've been so stupid," he groaned. "Those tubes aren't connected to a treasure hunt; they're made by termites. As they move around in mud and soil, termites create these tubes to protect themselves. They often make them on trees. And because I'm sure Tony Termite is involved in all of this, I reckon the tubes might lead us to the handover meeting place."

"Well, we've got forty minutes before midnight," shouted Itch. "Let's hurry!"

Twenty minutes later, Buzz and Itch had reached the end of the tube trail. They climbed to the top of a hill and there in front of them stood the gigantic W. J. Gubbins Sports Park.

"Do you think the mayor is being kept here?" asked Itch. "Because if you do, we'll *never* find him. This place is too big."

"We *have* to find him!" said Buzz.
"We can't let Sheriff Blatt hand over the
cash and we can't trust the kidnappers.
We *must* rescue the mayor!"

They hurried forward and went
through a small opening. It led directly
on to the stadium's pitch.

"Wow!" murmured Itch, as they
looked up at the huge seating stands.
"Where do we start?"

"You go left, I'll go right," said Buzz. "Work your way past every seat to see if Glug is being held in the stands. Let's go!"

The Fleatectives had never worked so fast. Speeding up and down the stands, they checked every seat and every exit. When they met up again they were standing at the very top of the stadium. It was three minutes before midnight.

"Looks like we've failed," said Itch miserably.

But at that moment there was a noise from the pitch. The fleas saw a tied-up figure lying on the grass.

"That's Mayor Glug!" cried Itch. He and Buzz raced down the steps, sprinted over the running track, jumped over the advertising boards and landed on the pitch.

"It's all right, Mayor Glug!" shouted Itch. "We're coming to save you!"

They raced over the pitch towards the mayor. But as they reached his side, they were grabbed from behind and shoved inside a short piece of transparent termite tubing. The two ends were lifted up and pressed together.

The Fleatectives were well and truly trapped!

Which Mayor Glug is
the odd one out?

A

B

C

D

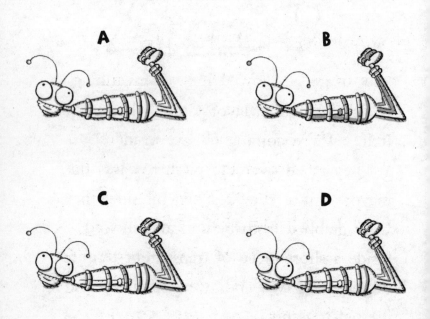

Answers at the back of the book

CHAPTER 8

"Let us go!" bellowed Itch. "This tubing is strictly for termites! We don't look like termites! We don't smell like termites! We're not termites and we never will be!"

FLEATASTIC FACT: Termites build their tubes out of plants, soil and spit! Sometimes the tubes can be several metres long.

The smirking face of Tony from the Cash and Carry Emporium appeared outside the tube.

"Thought you were clever, didn't you?" he cackled horribly.

"Fairly clever," replied Itch, "at least until this moment."

"In a couple of moments Sheriff Blatt will arrive with one million Bug Notes for us!" crowed Tony.

"Us?" asked Buzz.

Spicy Flaxton suddenly appeared.

"I knew you were involved!" snapped Buzz at the Dung Heap Café owner.

"Well, you were right!" said Spicy, "and now the idiot mayor has met his comeuppance!"

"Of course!" said Buzz, looking at Tony. "Those holes in the wooden walls of the mayor's office and his apartment were made by you, weren't they? They're termite holes. You were spying on him!"

"I'm very proud of my woodwork skills," smirked Tony.

"Hang on a second," said Itch, scratching his head. "*Why* did you kidnap the mayor? What's he ever done to you?"

"I have a very good idea why!" said Buzz, turning to Itch. "Do you remember the newspaper cutting from the *Larva Town Lancet* at the mayor's flat?"

Itch nodded.

"It was about Mayor Glug closing down the Dirt Shack restaurant because of food poisoning. I'll bet these two crooks owned that restaurant and they were so angry about it being shut down that they kidnapped the mayor."

"We *did* own it," snarled Spicy, "and we were doing very well."

"Only a few hundred insects got food

poisoning," said Tony.

"I get it!" cried Itch. "You started selling Mouldy Curl Chilli Snacks as a way to lure the mayor to your café so that you could kidnap him! Then you asked for one million Bug Notes so that you could open more restaurants."

"Got it in one," laughed Spicy. "We had to get the mayor out of the way. He was desperate for those snacks, so Tony got hold of some and sold them to me. When the mayor found out I had them, he started sneaking away from work and gobbling them up at my place."

"We waited until he'd visited us a few times and then we grabbed him!" cackled Tony.

"So that green spot on your body wasn't a tattoo; it was some skin flakes from the mayor!" marvelled Itch.

"I hate tattoos!" snapped Spicy.

"In one minute Sheriff Blatt will be here and we will be one million Bug Notes richer!" cried Tony.

"Then we'll be able to open up as many cafés and restaurants as we like and we'll get rid of the mayor so he won't be able to close any of them down!" yelled Spicy.

"It's a despicable plan!" shouted Itch.

"Unfortunately, you two won't be around to see it!" hissed Spicy. She grabbed one end of the termite tubing and she and Tony started to bend the ends even further towards each other. The Fleatectives felt the sides of the tube crushing them.

"This is it, dear friend!" said Itch. "They're going to totally squash the life out of us!"

But as Buzz unsuccessfully tried to push the two tube ends apart, Itch suddenly had an idea. He began to shake his body from side to side. He could just about manage this in the limited space.

"This really isn't the time for trying to fly!" shouted Buzz.

But Itch ignored him and increased his speed. In seconds he became a ball of energy. His body started forcing the two ends of the tube apart.

"Hey, what's going on?" demanded Tony.

Itch was now a wrecking ball. A couple of seconds later the two ends of the tube were smashed apart. Tony and Spicy were flung to the ground and Itch dived out of one of the now open ends.

"*Superb move!*" cried Buzz, leaping out of the hole after Itch.

"*HURRY!*" yelled Itch. He grabbed
Tony. Buzz nabbed Spicy. The
Fleatectives threw the two villains inside
the termite tube and quickly tied the
ends together. However hard they tried,
the crooks couldn't get out.

Buzz and Itch then ran over to the
mayor, untied him and gave him a few
slaps in the face to wake him up (Itch hit

him a bit harder than was necessary).

"W . . . w . . . what's going on?" murmured Mayor Glug, coming round.

He stood up and rubbed his sore head.

"You have *me* to thank for your rescue," declared Sheriff Blatt, appearing on the pitch.

"That's rubbish!" cried Itch. "It was *us* who got you out of this mess, Mr Mayor!"

"Ignore these amateurs," smiled Blatt. "Without me they wouldn't have had a clue what was going on."

"At least none of you thought about handing them the ransom money," said the mayor.

Sheriff Blatt gulped and quickly hid his suitcase behind his back – the suitcase that contained one million Bug Notes.

"I suggest we get these two criminals

to jail," said the mayor, "and then I can see what's been going on in my absence."

"Octavia and Cedric have held the fort very well," said Buzz. "They'll be delighted to get you back."

When they reached Sheriff Blatt's office they held up the termite tube and Tony and Spicy fell out. Before they could run away, Sheriff Blatt shoved them into the jail cell and locked the door.

Itch ran to get Cedric and Octavia, who wept with joy when they were reunited with the mayor.

"Anyone for an episode of *Cockroach Crime Crackers*?" asked the sheriff. "It's one of my favourite shows!"

"Don't mind if I do," smiled the mayor.

Cedric and Octavia declined, saying they had to get back to bed.

"As crime-crushing Fleatectives, we have no time for such leisure pursuits," said Buzz.

"Well, thanks again," smiled Mayor Glug. "Your help in this matter won't be forgotten."

"Their role in your rescue was truly

tiny compared to mine, Mayor," said
Sheriff Blatt.

"We did *loads* more than you!" shouted
Itch, as Blatt and the mayor went off to
the TV room.

"Come on," said Buzz, "let's go
home."

Itch was about to complain again, but
he remembered that he and Buzz had
just cracked another case in spectacular
fashion.

"Sorry about dragging you to the Web
Forest," said Buzz as they started off for
home.

"No problem," said Itch. "It was pretty
spooky in that hole, though, wasn't it?"

"I thought we might be stuck down
there for ever," smiled Buzz.

"Well, we weren't," grinned Itch,
"and one thing is going through my

mind right now."

"Don't tell me," said Buzz, "you're thinking about learning to fly?"

"No way!" grinned Itch. "I'm thinking, *bring on our next case!*"

Can you spot eight differences between these two pictures?

Answers at the back of the book

Yay, answers for our Fleatective puzzles!

Page 15

```
R Z A L F Z M Y K Q S A
I A E B A K J A K A M E
A M Y U G I Z U A E A P
B A T Z A D Z B I A Y X
C U X Z D N T A S H O O
H S G L R A N S O M R D
E G A N F P A U P R G A
P W L R Q A H O I A L N
K Y D U J T A I A B U A
J V Q K A M E C T W G O
A S M A N T I S A C A C
V F A W N X O B V G H Z
```

Page 41

1. HECTOR
2. DR BOPPER
3. MOULDY CURL CHILLI SNACKS
4. DUNG HEAP CAFE
5. MAYOR GLUG
6. FLEATECTIVES

Page 28

Key A opens Lock 2
Key B opens Lock 3
Key C opens Lock 1

Page 56

Spicy 'D'

Page 67

START

FINISH

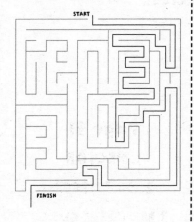

Page 94

Mayor 'B'

Page 85

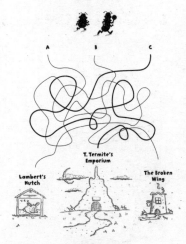

A   B   C

Lambert's
Hutch

T. Termite's
Emporium

The Broken
Wing

Path 'C'

Page 109

Have you read?

All the nectar in Larva Town
has gone missing!
The West Side bees say it's
the East Side bees, but are
either of them really to blame?
It's up to the Fleatectives
to find the culprit.

CHAPTER 1

It was a warm early evening in Larva Town's West Side Wood and the sun was throwing lengthening shadows on the ground. A caterpillar was snoring on a nearby leaf, and a family of maggots were being made filthy by their mother.

It had been a quiet day for Buzz and Itch's newly founded Fleatectives Crime-Crushing Agency. In fact, every day was quiet, as the number of cases they'd managed to pick up so far was . . . zero.

Itch was jumping across an area of smooth mud and muttering to himself.

Buzz looked up from last month's copy of *Insect Crime Monthly* (this month's had mysteriously gone missing). "What are you doing?" he asked his crime-crushing partner.

"Trying to fly," replied Itch.

"How many times do I have to tell you?" Buzz sighed, wiggling his antennae with frustration. "We're FLEAS. We don't have wings so we don't fly!"

"But I could be the first flying flea," replied Itch, looking hopeful. He was about to carry on with his flying project when two thorax-shaking shrieks rang through the wood.

"THE WEST SIDE HIVE NEVER TAKES MORE THAN IT NEEDS!"

"THE EAST SIDE HIVE WOULD NEVER DREAM OF STEALING!"

"What's that about?" asked Itch.

"We'd better go and investigate," replied Buzz.

The two of them hurried past a line of twigs and arrived at the source of the outburst. Two female honeybees were standing compound-eye to compound-eye on a jagged pebble, bawling at each other.

One had the light brown stripes of the local West Side hive bees. The other's stripes were darker, indicating she was from the East Side hive.

"THIEF!"

"ROBBER!"

"Ladies, LADIES!" exclaimed Buzz, striding over and placing his tiny frame between them. "What seems to be the problem?"

"Not that it's any of your business," snapped the West Side bee, looking down at him, "but the entire West Side of town is totally nectar free; there's not a drop of it anywhere. And that's because *her* lot from the East Side have been encroaching into our air space and taking what's NOT THEIRS!"

"That is absolute RUBBISH!" hissed her opponent. "The only reason I've travelled here from the East Side is because we have no nectar in *our* zone. We reckon it's the West Side posse who have filched the lot."

"How DARE you!" screamed the West Sider.

"OH I DARE!" hollered the East Sider.

"Maybe they've been taking *each other's* nectar," suggested Itch.

Who stole the nectar?

Read
CASE OF THE STOLEN NECTAR
to find out!

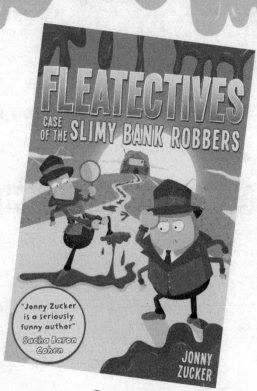